HER NORTH POI
BY
STACY-DEANNE

Stacy-Deanne

BOOKS FOR YOUR SOUL

Readers: Thanks so much for choosing my book! I would be very appreciative if you would leave reviews when you are done. Much love!

Email: stacydeanne1@aol.com
Website: Stacy's Website [1]
Facebook: Stacy's Facebook Profile[2]
Twitter: Stacy's Twitter[3]

To receive book announcements subscribe to Stacy's mailing list:

Mailing List[4]

---

1.   https://www.stacy-deanne.com/

2.   https://www.facebook.com/stacy.deanne.5

3.   https://twitter.com/stacydeanne

4.   https://stacybooks.eo.page/cjjy6

CHAPTER ONE

Sherry Rice sat at her cluttered desk as the newsroom buzzed around her.

She sighed, stroking her long auburn braids as she stared at the blinking cursor on the half-finished story about a lost cat.

How did it come to this?

She had dreams of breaking big stories, of exposing corruption and changing the world. Instead, she was stuck writing fluff pieces that hardly got any clicks.

She scanned the newsroom, seeing her colleagues at the *Dallas Daily* engaged in serious discussions and wondering what the hell she'd been doing at this joke of a paper for the last three years.

"Hey, girl."

Nina McMillian, Sherry's best friend of ten years and fellow reporter, leaned against Sherry's desk, holding two cups of coffee.

It was impossible not to notice Nina with her high yellow skin and long, curly black weave with purple highlights. She exuded a fun and bold energy, reflected in her fierce fashion choices. From over-the-top fake nails painted with glitter and gold streaks to the bright makeup slathered over her round face, Nina's style would've been tacky on anyone else, but she made it work.

"Man, it's hot today, goodness." Nina passed Sherry a cup. "It's winter and it's still eighty-something degrees. How's the story going?"

"Just peachy." Sherry rolled her eyes as she blew into her coffee cup. "Another riveting tale of Mr. Whiskers going missing in the suburbs. This is Pulitzer material, girl. If you didn't know, now you do."

Nina smirked, crossing her long legs. "Hey, it could be worse. At least you're

not covering the bake sale at the senior center again."

"Thank God for small favors."

"I'm sick of you in this funk. I mean, you're always moody, but you're worse this week."

"I'm just tired." Sherry stretched. "I'm sick of chasing stories that don't matter. Look at this crap. We write about cats, traffic, and who won the latest bingo competition. It's pathetic, Nina. Dallas is too damn big of a place for this paper to be so crappy."

"All the good stuff goes to *The Dallas Morning News*. We're just a little teeny community paper who gets the stuff the *real* paper doesn't wanna cover."

"Well, I'm sick of picking over scraps. We didn't graduate journalism school to be writing about toe fungus and potholes." Sherry sat forward. "We got into this to make a difference, you know? Remember our dream, Nina? We were gonna start our own newspaper. Think about it. Two sistas running their own paper the way they want and we'd be covering the good stuff too. Exclusives. Heck, when I took this job I thought it would allow me to grow but I've been here three years and Ms. Ray doesn't even trust me enough to give me an exclusive and when I come to her with a real story, she brushes me off. She doesn't treat me like a serious journalist."

"Maybe this is *my* fault." Nina batted her false lashes. "I'm the one who told you to apply here, but it's only holding you back."

"It's holding you back, too."

"Nah, I'm good." Nina shrugged. "Might sound crazy, but I enjoy working here. I thought I wanted the big time, writing for some New York paper. But, guess the comfort's got to me and not sure I wanna risk what I got going on. But you, Sherry, you're too good for this place." Nina leaned over and patted Sherry's hand. "It's just a

matter of time before you catch a break. I can feel it."

"You're right!" Sherry slapped the papers on her desk. "What am I doing sitting here whining like a baby? *I'm* the ruler of my future, aren't I? If I don't like where I'm at, I gotta do something about it. I don't think this break is ever gonna come with me writing *here*. No." She looked out of the window behind her desk. "It's a big world out there just waiting for me, Nina. If I'm gonna get my big break, I gotta take it!" She stood. "I'm gonna go talk to Ms. Ray right now and demand she give me a real story or I'm leaving."

"Ha, ha, yeah!" Nina jumped off the desk. "That's the spirit. You're a damn good reporter, Sherry, and if she doesn't realize that after three years, she probably never will."

"Oh, she's gonna realize it." Sherry pulled at her black pencil skirt while eying the glass door of Ms. Ray's office. "I'm gonna make sure she does if it kills me. I'm gonna go talk to her right—"

Ms. Ray flung her door open. "Rice! My office. Now!"

Everyone paused and looked up at Sherry, whose heart skipped a million beats.

"Oh, God." Sherry fell back into her chair, then jumped back up. "Shoot, shoot, shoot! What do I do?" She grabbed Nina. "You think she heard me? What do I do?"

"Girl, I know you're not going out like this with all that big talk you were just doing." Nina straightened her back like a soldier. "Everything you just told me, go tell her and if she doesn't listen, give her your notice."

"Yeah." Sherry smoothed her skirt, and sauntered into Ms. Ray's office.

"Sit down, Sherry." Ms. Ray motioned for Sherry to sit in the chair across her desk.

As the founder of the *Dallas Daily*, Ms. Ray commanded the place like the

boss she was and didn't give two hoots if you liked it or not.

A striking white woman with delicate features and a youthful appearance

despite being in her early 60s, Ms. Yvonne Ray stood at medium-height, her slender figure always accentuated by the stylish cut of her designer skirt suits. Her silvery-gray hair was fashioned in a chic pixie cut, adding to her aura of sophisticated elegance reminiscent of one of Sherry's favorite actresses, Glenn Close.

Ms. Ray cleared her throat as she set her document aside. "You've been here for how long now?"

"Three years."

Ms. Ray nodded. "And you've been reliable, consistent. You do good work."

"Thank you, ma'am." Sherry couldn't help but feel like there was a "but" coming.

Ms. Ray's gaze softened. "I'm aware you've been frustrated lately, feeling like your talents are being underutilized. You're ambitious, and I can respect that. That's why I'm giving you an opportunity. An exclusive assignment. One that could put your name on the map."

Sherry jerked forward. "What is it?"

Ms. Ray pulled a slim folder out of her desk drawer and slid it to Sherry.

Sherry scanned the label: "North Pole—Santa Claus Exclusive." She blinked, wondering if she was seeing things. "Is this... some kind of joke?"

"No joke." Ms. Ray sat back, clasping her hands in her lap. "We've been presented with a unique opportunity. Santa Claus has agreed to an interview, and you're the one I'm sending to get it."

Sherry stared at her boss, waiting for her to crack a smile or laugh. But Ms. Ray's expression remained stony.

"Let me get this straight." Sherry chuckled. "You want me to go to the North Pole and interview Santa Claus? Am I the crazy one, or are you?"

Ms. Ray chuckled. "Isn't this what you wanted? Rice, you'll go where no reporter ever has and get an inside look at the man behind the legend. How he operates, his life, his thoughts on Christmas in the modern world. And you'll have exclusive access."

Thoughts flooded Sherry's mind, each one competing for her attention and causing her heart to beat faster.

An interview with Old St. Nick?

No one else would have this story. If Sherry could pull it off, Gayle King would

be contacting *her* and begging for a job.

"Wow, Ms. Ray! I'm flattered, but why *me*?"

"Because you deserve it, and because I think you need it. A change of scenery, something different to spark that fire again."

Sherry looked down at the folder in her hands, then back at Ms. Ray. "When do I leave?"

"Friday, that's in four days. The arrangements have been made. Pack warm, and be ready to write the story of your life. I'm giving you the next few days off so you can prepare. You've got a big adventure ahead."

Sherry nodded, her head filled with a whirlwind of emotions that she couldn't quite grasp. "I won't let you down."

Ms. Ray raised an eyebrow. "You better not. You get *one* big chance to prove yourself in this field, Sherry, and this one's *yours*."

CHAPTER TWO

The biting cold hit Sherry the moment she stepped off the plane. Her breath puffed out in white clouds as she pulled her coat tighter around herself, trying to ward off the chill.

The North Pole was everything she'd imagined it would be: a sea of white, snow blanketing everything in sight, with a silvery-gray sky. It was a real-life winter wonderland, but Sherry couldn't shake the nervous flutter in her stomach as she took in the enchanting surroundings.

A tall pale man in a green wool coat and fur-lined boots approached, holding a sign that read, "Sherry Rice—*Dallas Daily*." His jet-black beard and lively brown eyes seemed out of place in the cold, stern environment.

"Ms. Rice?" He waved, his voice deep and warm.

"Oh, hello!" Sherry rushed to him, offering her hand. "You must be—"

"Barnaby." The man laughed, taking her hand in a firm grip. "I'm Nick's operations manager. I'll be your guide during your stay."

Sherry clenched her teeth together to keep them from chattering. "Nice to meet you, Barnaby. Thanks for meeting me here."

Barnaby nodded, grabbing her suitcases. "Let's get you to the workshop. The cold here takes some getting used to. Must be quite a change to you coming from Dallas."

"Yeah, well, most don't know it, but we get pretty chilly winters in Dallas, too." Sherry followed Barnaby out of the tiny airport, trudging through the thick snow in her brand new designer boots.

Barnaby led her to a sleek, snow-covered sleigh, the kind Sherry had only seen

in Christmas movies. The polished wood glistened in the muted sunlight, and the soft

cushions clasped her butt as she took a seat.

At Barnaby's gentle command, a reindeer with an impressive set of antlers, trotted forward, and the sleigh glided over the powdery snow, leaving a trail of tiny hoof prints behind them.

Sherry reveled in the landscape as they traveled. The hills stretched out in every direction, broken only by the occasional pine tree or snowdrift.

It was beautiful yet intimidating because it reminded her she was far from home.

"Is it always this quiet?"

Barnaby wriggled. "Most of the time. But things will get busier the closer we get to Christmas. The elves work around the clock, and there's a lot of activity in the village."

Sherry chuckled. "Let me guess, I'm the only black person in Santa's Village, right?"

"Well, *no*." Barnaby raised his eyebrows. "There's Chester, the mailman."

"Just me and old Chester, huh?" Sherry concentrated on the beauty before her. "Of course I've seen pictures of the North Pole and read stories but didn't know it was this amazing. How do you guys concentrate on work living in a place so amazing? Don't you get distracted?"

"We get time off, but the children are the most important, so we make sure we work throughout the year to have all the toys ready for the sweet little boys and girls. Without them, what would be the reason for all of this?"

Being a reporter, naturally, Sherry's curiosity got the better of her. "So, how has Nick been doing? I mean, *really* doing?"

Barnaby fidgeted. "Well, he's been in a bit of a slump. Ever since Mrs. Claus

divorced him—"

"Yeah, she ran off with that elf, right?"

"It hit him hard. They were together for centuries, and to see it end like that... It's not something you just bounce back from. He's always been the one to spread joy, but now, he's the one who needs it. He's been distant, not just with the work, but with everyone around him."

"That's awful, but why did he agree to do the story? I mean, it seems like the last thing he'd want is a reporter poking around in his life."

"At first, he didn't want to. He was adamant about not letting anyone in, not letting the world see how things are right now. But then something changed."

"What?"

Barnaby took a deep breath. "Nick agreed because of the kids. After everything that happened, he's been questioning his place in all of this—whether he's still the right person to be Santa, to bring joy to children around the world. He feels like he's lost touch with what made it all special. But then he realized that maybe, just maybe, opening up to someone like you could help him find that spark again. He thinks that if he can be honest, not just with you but with himself, then maybe he can rediscover the joy he once had in the work he does."

Sherry pondered the thoughtful explanation. "So, it's not just about the story. It's about him trying to find his way back to who he used to be."

"He's hoping that by letting you in, by showing the world the real Nick, he might reconnect with that part of himself that's been buried under all this sadness. He's trying to heal, in his own way."

"I was just thinking about how this story would benefit *me*, but it's so much more to it than that."

"It is. And that's why he's going to need your help, Miss Sherry. He doesn't just need someone to write a story; he needs someone to remind him of who he is, and someone who can see the good in him, even when he can't see it himself."

Sherry whimpered as a deep sense of responsibility landed on her shoulders. "I'll do my best. For Nick, and for the kids who believe in him."

Barnaby smiled. "I've got a good feeling about you. And so will Nick, even if he won't admit it."

They continued through the landscape with Shelly focusing on the task ahead.

She wasn't just here for a story anymore—she was here to help Nick find his way back to the man he once was, the man the world needed him to be.

They reached the top of the hill. The village stretched out below, straight out of a storybook. Each house dripped with colorful icicle lights and decorative gingerbread trimmings. Everything smelled of fresh pine and cinnamon and the faint sound of jingle bells only added to the whimsical atmosphere.

"Welcome to Santa's Village!" Barnaby howled.

"It's... beautiful."

Barnaby guided the sleigh through the village, past bustling elves who waved as they passed. They were tiny, only three feet tall, with pointed ears and bright, cheery faces. Some were carrying stacks of presents, others were busy hanging decorations or trimming trees. It was what Sherry had imagined as a child, but seeing it in person was surreal.

They arrived at a colorful two-story log cabin in the heart of the North Pole.

The structure was divided into Santa's workshop and his home.

The emerald green shutters contrasted beautifully with the red door, giving the building a charming and eye-catching appearance.

Twinkling fairy lights made the roof sparkle and candy cane-striped columns bordered the porch, where festive wreaths hung.

The front door swung open, and a young elf with curly hair and a mischievous grin bounded down the steps.

"Barnaby! You're back!" The elf spotted Sherry and gasped. "Is this the journalist? Oh wow, oh wow, this is so cool! And she's pretty too!"

Sherry tucked in her grin as Barnaby chuckled.

"Calm down, Pip," Barnaby said. "Yes, this is Miss Sherry Rice, and we need to make her stay as pleasant as possible while she's here."

"When's the interview?" Pip jumped up and down, gaping. "Now? Like, right now?"

"Aren't you just a ball of energy? I suggest less candy and more decaf," Sherry joked.

"I'll go tell Santa you're here!" Pip clapped. "He's always grumpy these days, but maybe you'll cheer him up!"

He dashed inside, leaving the door ajar.

Barnaby jumped out of the sleigh and got Sherry's bags. "Let me show you to your room. You'll want to freshen up before you meet him."

Sherry followed Barnaby into the workshop, which was even more impressive on the inside. Rows of workbenches filled the large space, with elves working on toys, gadgets, and gizmos.

A lively buzz filled the air, accompanied by the sweet and spicy scent of cinnamon and peppermint.

Barnaby led Sherry down a hallway to a cozy guest room decorated in rich reds and greens, with a gigantic bed covered in a quilt that looked handmade.

A small fire crackled in the corner, filling the room with warmth.

"Well, this is your room. Hope it suits you." Barnaby let out an exhausted groan

as he set her suitcases down on the Christmas rug. "Nick will meet with you later today. In the meantime, get settled."

"Thank you very much, and the room is lovely."

Barnaby smiled as he walked out, closing the door behind him.

Sherry sat on the edge of the bed and still couldn't believe she was here, at the North Pole, about to meet Santa Claus and have the interview of her lifetime.

CHAPTER THREE

Sherry didn't know what to expect as she walked down the hall toward Santa's office. Barnaby had told her to wait until she was called, so she stood outside the heavy wooden door, fidgeting with her notepad.

The door creaked open, and Pip's head popped out. "He's ready for you!"

Sherry took a deep breath and stepped inside.

The room was nothing like she'd imagined. Instead of a grand office filled with holiday decorations and cheerful trinkets, it was more like a study. The walls were covered in dark wood paneling and the shelves were lined with old books.

A large, weathered desk sat in the middle, papers scattered across it, and behind it sat Santa Claus—only he didn't look like Santa.

Gone was the jolly man with rosy cheeks and a twinkle in his eye. Instead, Sherry saw a man who looked weary, almost haggard.

His thick hair sparkled with whiteness, but it was tangled, and his beard looked like it hadn't been trimmed in weeks. He wore a red sweater that sagged on his hefty frame, and his expression was one of irritation rather than cheer.

Nick squinted, his brows knitting together in a sharp frown. "So, you're the journalist."

"Yes, sir. I'm Sherry Rice, from the *Dallas Daily Newspaper*. Thank you for agreeing to meet with me."

"Didn't have much of a choice." He wiggled his red nose. "You're not what I pictured. Much younger than I thought you'd be."

"I'm thirty-two."

"I didn't wanna do this, you know?" A hint of admiration flashed through his

eyes before he covered it up with a scowl. "But sometimes stepping out of our comfort zones is necessary in order to grow. And when we grow, we get better. Don't you

agree?"

Sherry presented a shaky smile. "I appreciate you doing this, believe me. I'd like to learn more about your life here, the work you do, and... anything you'd like to share."

Nick leaned back in his chair, wiggling his snow-white mustache as he studied her. "You want to know about my life, huh? Well, it's not as magical as you might think. My wife left me. The elves are on the verge of a strike. And I'm running out of ideas to keep kids interested in Christmas."

"I... I'm sorry to hear that."

"Yeah, everyone thinks it's all fun and games. Like being Santa Claus is easy, but it's a job like any other, and it's wearing me down."

"Why don't we break the ice before jumping into the interview? Maybe that would make you more comfortable."

Nick rolled his eyes.

"How about you show me around?" Sherry held her notepad to her bosom. "I could get a better sense of what you do."

"Fine." Nick exhaled as he got up. "Let's get this over with."

He stood at a towering height of 6 feet and 6 inches, and his massive physique and long limbs seemed to go on for miles. Sherry had always prided herself on her 5'7" stature, but next to Nick, *she* felt like an elf.

The top of his head was bald, surrounded by long locks that flowed down his body like a shimmering waterfall of silver. You couldn't tell where his hair stopped and his beard began.

He looked like a lion, strong and commanding with his majestic mane and

regal posture.

"Wow." Sherry stared up at him like a kid getting ready to climb a tree. "You're *big*. I mean, I knew you were, but it's something to see in person."

"Shall we?" Nick walked out of the office, shaking the wood floor, his shoulders hunched as if the weight of the world rested on them.

They reached the workshop, and Sherry's earlier awe returned as she saw the elves at work again, assembling toys with remarkable speed and precision.

"This is where the magic happens," Nick muttered, no enthusiasm in his voice.

"We make toys, we pack them, I deliver them on Christmas Eve. Rinse and repeat."

An elf painted the details on a toy train, the craftsmanship impeccable.

"It's incredible," Sherry said. "It must be rewarding, seeing the joy these toys bring to kids."

Nick gave a half-hearted shrug. "It used to be. Now, it's just routine."

Before Sherry could inquire, Pip appeared again, bouncing on his toes. "Nick! The reindeer are ready for their evening feed. Should I take care of it?"

"No, I'll do it. Ms. Rice can come along."

Pip beamed at Sherry. "You're gonna love this. The reindeer are the best!"

Sherry smiled, though Nick's demeanor still rattled her. "I'd love to see them."

Nick led the way to the stables. The smell of hay and the soft sounds of the animals made the space feel almost peaceful.

Sherry's eyes widened as she saw the famous reindeer, each with a nameplate above their stall. "They're beautiful."

One reindeer, a majestic creature with thick fur and kind eyes, nuzzled her hand as she reached out to touch him.

Nick watched her, his eyes filled with a hint of tenderness. "They're the best

part of this job. They don't ask for much, just some food and care, and they love me unconditionally." Nick dropped his gaze while clearing his throat. "Let's get them fed."

They got to work, filling the troughs with hay and grain. The reindeer gathered, snorting and nibbling.

As they finished up, Sherry smiled at Nick. "Thank you for letting me help. I know this isn't easy for you. Letting a stranger into your world."

"And now that you've gotten a glimpse of it..." Nick leaned his hefty body

against the stall, causing it to creak under his weight. "Are you disappointed?"

She got up off her knees and dusted the hay from her hands. "Why should I be disappointed?"

"Oh, to see that underneath it all, I'm just a man like any other man. No special powers to cure the world. Heck..." The sparkle disappeared from his pale-blue eyes. "I can't even cure myself."

Sherry's heart ached at his words. She'd come here expecting to meet a legend, but she found a man struggling with his own humanity. "Maybe that's what people need to see. That even Santa Claus has hard times."

Nick met her gaze, and for the first time since they'd met, there was a flicker of something in his eyes—maybe understanding, maybe something else. "Maybe."

They stood there for a moment, the warmth of the stables wrapping around them like a comforting blanket.

Sherry didn't know what would happen next, but she knew one thing: she was

beginning to see the real Nick, and she felt that was where the true story lay.

CHAPTER FOUR

Sherry woke up the next morning to the sound of sleigh bells jingling outside her window.

She stretched, feeling the comforting warmth of the fire that had kept her room cozy through the night. For a moment, she forgot where she was, but the sight of the snow-covered village outside brought everything back.

She dressed, choosing a thick sweater and jeans, then headed out to find Nick.

Elves scurried about, preparing for the final push before Christmas Eve.

Sherry marveled at their efficiency, but she couldn't help but notice that some of them glanced at her with curious, almost wary eyes.

She found Barnaby overseeing a group of elves who were decorating a large Christmas tree in the village square.

The enormous tree stood tall, its branches reaching out with a lush greenness and a dazzling display of twinkling lights and ornaments in all shapes and sizes.

"Good *morning*, Miss Rice!" Barnaby's booming voice reverberated, capturing everyone's attention. "How did you sleep?"

"Like a log." Sherry yawned. "So good, I forgot where I was. How's Nick doing today?"

Barnaby's gaze drifted towards the workshop, his shoulders slumped. "He's... well, he's trying. Even though he agreed to the interview, it's still a change having you here. We never have visitors at the North Pole."

"He's feeling vulnerable, I get it. But isn't that the point?" Sherry bounced on her boots. "He feels it's important to let everyone in, so he has to put his big Santa pants on and do it."

Barnaby gaped. "Are you planning on talking to Nick like this?"

"If I have to, sure. He's got a lot going for him and can't just sit around sulking."

She held her hips. "Besides, this is all for the kids, right? They deserve to know the man behind the beard and the jolly "ho-ho-hos.""

He chuckled. "One thing's for sure, Miss Sherry, there won't be a dull moment with *you* around. Nick's in the stables, by the way."

Grinning, Sherry tottered through the snow and as she approached the stables,

heard the familiar sound of reindeer hooves on the straw-covered floor and the soft murmur of Nick's voice.

She hesitated for a moment before stepping inside.

Nick stood in front of a stall, brushing the reindeer's thick fur. He seemed to know Sherry was there, but didn't look her way.

"Morning." Sherry pushed her hands into her pockets. "You slept okay?"

"I should be asking you that, shouldn't I?" Nick's tone remained neutral. "After all, you're our guest."

"I had the best sleep of my life!" She laughed, twirling around with her arms out. "Sorry."

"For what?"

"For acting so silly, but that's what this place does to you." She stepped closer to him. "I'm not just interested in the village, Nick. I want to know more about *you*. Everything. That's the point of this story, remember?" She whipped out her notepad and pencil.

He snickered, his fat rosy cheeks spreading. "Something tells me you never go

anywhere without that thing. Kinda old-fashioned, isn't it? Why not just use the recorder on your cellphone?"

"Look who's talking?" Sherry scoffed, sitting on a block of hay. "The same man

who still writes on a scroll."

"Oh, please. I don't write on a *scroll*." He scratched under his brown beanie cap. "I haven't used that thing in a century."

"Then why is it all open on your desk, as if you were just using it before I got here?"

He tucked in his grin. "That was to impress you. I had to live up to the hype, right? I didn't want your ideas of me dashed if you knew I'd been using my iPhone to keep up with everything. Thought you'd might find it lazy."

She laughed. "You have an iPhone?"

"Well, duh. What? You think I don't keep up with the times? Didn't you notice the computers and the technology I've infused in this place?"

"Of course, but I thought that was just to keep business running smoothly." She crossed her legs, staring at him in awe. "I didn't think you used that stuff."

"Just because I'm old doesn't mean I can't stay with the times. My iPhone has been a blessing." He clasped his gloved hands over his pot belly. "I use it to schedule my Christmas deliveries, and I have a list of all the kids in the world in alphabetical order with their addresses, phone numbers, and email addresses. I also have my Naughty List on there, too." He grinned, his cheeks spreading. "Makes it so much easier than a notebook to keep up with who's been naughty and who's been nice."

Sherry laughed.

"And I guess when you were a kid, you still just wrote me letters, right?"

She nodded. "Yep. Every year, I'd sit down and write you this long three or four-page letter and send it off."

"These days, the kids email me or use my app."

"Wait, a darn minute here." Sherry dropped her shoulders. "You have an app?"

"Yeah, girl. Let me show you." Nick took out his iPhone and showed her his app. "With this, kids can contact me any time. All they have to do is fill out their profile and type what they want for Christmas. They can even upload pictures of items or paste in links to toys to make sure I bring 'em the right thing."

"Well, I'll be darn." Sherry gaped, experimenting with the app. "I'm jealous heck! Man, if I'd had this when I was a kid, oh you'd had *no* peace."

Chuckling, Nick took his phone back. "Believe me, I know. This one little girl, Jamie... oh." He rolled his eyes. "She contacts me every single day to remind me not to forget her at Christmas. As if anyone could forget *her*."

Sherry laughed. "Wow, a Santa app. Yep, me and my friend Nina would've been blowing you up when we were kids."

"No matter what I'm doing or how I'm feeling, I want the kids to know I'm always there for them." He put his phone up. "They're what matters."

"Tell me about when you first got started." Sherry readied her pencil to write.

"When you first became Santa."

"Woo." Nick whistled. "It was so long ago, I don't even remember. Guess you can say it was my calling and God blessed me to be the man who was in charge of the Christmas Spirit."

"What makes you happiest about being Santa Claus?"

Nick's eyes sparkled with delight, brightening up his face. "The joy, the

magic, and the wonder in children's eyes. It's everything I could have hoped for."

As soon as he got those words out, the glimmer of optimism that had briefly illuminated his face disappeared.

"What's wrong, Nick?"

"I spend my life making children's dreams come true, making them happy, but

I couldn't even make my wife happy." He walked toward the stalls. "Gertrude was my rock, the one who kept me grounded. When she ran off with Brutus, I didn't think I could do this anymore. Not without her."

"I'm so sorry, Nick. I can imagine how hard this is. May I ask why she left?"

"Same old story, and it was my fault. For decades she'd felt neglected because I spend every day leading up to Christmas Eve working on toys, overseeing Christmas lists, keeping up with the kids. I never had time for her. So what happens?" He shrugged. "She turned to another man. Granted, a much, much smaller man in size, but what he lacked in height he gave with his heart." He rubbed his gloved hands together. "She didn't even have to tell me. I knew what was going on before they ran off. Every night, Gertie used to get out of bed and sneak down to the workshop to be with Brutus. Then, she started making peanut brownies every day."

"Um, how did *that* prove she was cheating?"

"Brutus is the only elf who wasn't allergic to peanuts."

"Oh." Sherry gaped. "I guess that would give it away."

"And the way he was always looking at my Gertie and she'd be blushing and giggling. Didn't take a rocket scientist to figure it out. Even the other elves knew it. Well, I guess it's not so much her running away as me *pushing* her away."

"Where are they now?"

"Cleveland. Can you believe that?" He grimaced. "She goes off, leaves Santa's

Village for *Cleveland*? Who goes to Cleveland on purpose? Anyway, I'm over her now.

If she wants Brutus, I wish her well."

"But you two were together for so long."

"Yeah, well, those are the breaks." He stood against the wall. "I don't want anyone to be with me if they don't wanna be."

"I can't see how any woman wouldn't wanna be with Santa Claus."

He squinted at her and she noticed something new in his expression.

His hard exterior melted away, revealing a vulnerability that tugged at her heartstrings.

Despite not being her usual type physically, Nick's gentle and empathetic nature drew her to him. It didn't matter that he was older than time itself, had a belly like he was 20 months pregnant, and was hairier than Big Foot. What captivated her was the goodness in his character and the fire in his soul.

CHAPTER FIVE

"So." Nick bounced with a twinkle in his eye. "Do the questions only go one way or do I get to know more about *you*?"

Heat spread across Sherry's cheeks. "Um, what do you want to know?"

He pushed up his glasses. "Anything."

"My family's from Houston but we moved to Dallas when I was a newborn. I have a brother named Shawn and a sister named Sheila. I'm the baby." She chuckled. "My mom was a schoolteacher, and my dad was a mechanic. Both are retired now. We lived a pretty good life. Decent, middle-class neighborhood and us kids never wanted for anything."

Nick relaxed his posture, holding a small smile.

"Christmas was always special for us, and no matter what was going on, my parents made sure we never missed out on the magic. A big part of that magic was you, of course." Sherry couldn't help but giggle at the way he stared at her, his gaze filled with adoration. "I believed in you with all my heart. Even when some people spread that myth that you weren't real, I knew the truth. I felt you in my heart, like all the other kids. You gave me my Christmas spirit, and for that, I'll always be grateful."

Sincerity shone through Nick's smile, illuminating his entire face.

Sherry squeezed her pencil while bouncing her leg. "I guess that's part of why I became a reporter. Growing up, I saw how much a story could affect people, how it could inspire or bring change. I wanted to be a part of that. But it hasn't been easy. This job... it's tough. I've had to fight for every scrap of recognition and still haven't gotten where I wanna be. But maybe that'll change." She smiled. "After this story."

"Hmm. What about relationships? *Romantic* relationships?"

She jerked up with a gasp. In her wildest dreams, she never thought she'd be having *this* conversation with Santa Claus.

"I've had my share of relationships, but they never lasted. Most guys didn't understand why I was so driven, why I cared so much about my work. They saw it as competition, something that kept me from them." She looked down at the worn wood beneath her feet. "So, I've been alone for a while. I figured if I focused on my career, I'd get that big break and everything would fall into place. But... it's been harder than I thought."

"Why are you so sure doing my story will get you where you wanna be?"

"Because it's not just about the story, Nick. It's about finding that magic again. The magic that made me believe in something bigger than myself. I thought that maybe, if I could tell your story—the big story—it might help me find what I've been missing, too."

"Well..." Nick struggled to scratch his chin through the denseness of his beard. "Looks like we have more in common than I thought."

"Yeah." Sherry smiled, warmth flooding through her. "I guess we do."

****

The next few days passed in a blur of snow, laughter, and fun. Each morning, Sherry and Nick would meet for breakfast in the cozy dining hall, where Dida, a female elf who was the head chef of the village, insisted on feeding them a steady diet

of pancakes, hot cocoa, and cinnamon rolls.

Sherry would grumble about the pounds she'd probably gain, but the food was

just as magical as everything else, so it was impossible to turn it away.

Nick was a junk food junkie who ate so many sweets that if you cut his wrist, sugar would fall out. And when Sherry would tease him about it, he'd pat his round belly and say, 'Gotta keep up the good ole' physique!', making her laugh so hard she almost fell out of her chair.

After breakfast, they'd head out to different parts of the village.

Sherry learned how the elves coordinated the global gift deliveries, using Santa's own app that showed every child's location in real time. No matter how much time she spent there, Sherry remained surprised at how smoothly the elves kept the operation running.

Nick never had to oversee them much or get on them if they made mistakes because no one ever seemed to make them. Then again, when you've been doing something for centuries like the elves, it became second nature.

The elves were a lively, colorful bunch, each with their own quirks and talents.

There was Ginger, the cookie decorator, who could paint the Mona Lisa on a gingerbread man; Jingle, the workshop foreman, who spoke in rapid-fire sentences that Sherry struggled to keep up with; and Tinsel, the female hairdresser and village gossip, who seemed to know everything about everyone, including Sherry and Nick.

"They make a cute couple, don't they?" Sherry would overhear Tinsel whispering to different elves every time she and Nick went out together.

Now, on the surface, the idea seemed beyond silly. Sherry Rice and Santa Claus being a *couple*?

Sherry had always admired Nick, but never had she ever thought of him as

"dating material." But that seemed to change, and Sherry had no control. It was

funny, but despite his moodiness, Nick had everything she looked for in a man.

Santa may not be your typical catch, but the man was top-notch mating

material. He had an amazing work ethic, and discipline. The guy delivered presents

all around the world in one night and in all the centuries of doing it he had never

missed not one Christmas. Sherry had dated men that either didn't wanna work or would call in sick if they had an ingrown toenail.

Nick had a gentle spirit that allowed him to understand others deeply. Shelly's exes, never listened. They just sat there while she poured out her feelings, grunting a few times to make her think they were listening while they were just waiting for her to shut up so they could get back to watching the Cowboys' game.

Nick actually listened to her and seemed to breathe in every word she said.

Sherry even found him attractive now. She loved his belly - soft and round like a giant marshmallow. While walking with him, she'd always pretend to trip and purposely bump into him so she could get a quick rub of his stomach. She wondered what he would look like without all that white hair and beard, but it added to his charm. The snowy-white strands and his rosy cheeks made him even more handsome, a doorway to the warm smile that always light up his face.

So, despite the whole living in the North Pole thing and that he was a million years older than Sherry, Nick had some pretty relatable qualities that would make any woman think he's a keeper.

Well, except for *Mrs.* Claus, obviously. Ouch.

****

One afternoon, Nick took Sherry's hand and led her through the hectic village,

their boots leaving deep imprints in the fresh snow.

He gave a backstory on the quaint shops and colorful buildings as they headed

to a small hill just outside the main square.

Sherry pulled her coat tighter around her, the frosty air stinging her cheeks.

When they perched the hill, Nick pointed towards a group of reindeer in the

distance. "Watch this." He bellowed to the reindeer, "Why don't you show Sherry how

well you can fly?"

The reindeer sprang into action, their muscles propelling them forward with graceful strides. Powerful hooves churned up snow, leaving a trail of sparkling powder behind them.

Sherry gasped as the animals soared through the air with ease.

The gentle tinkle of bells echoed through the forest, adding even more magic to the moment.

"This is where it all happens!" Nick threw his arms out, his belly bouncing as he belted out a booming, "Ho, ho, ho!"

Sherry laughed, covering her ears. "This is where you take off on Christmas Eve?"

Nick nodded, pointing. "The reindeer line up, we harness them to the sleigh, and then... we flyyyyyyyy!"

"It must be incredible to be soaring over the world like that." She clasped her gloved hands. "Since being a kid, I dreamed of riding with you on Christmas Eve as you delivered toys. I wished every year that you'd come take me away. Well, I'm sure every kid does, though."

Nick touched her chin, lifting it until she looked at him. "Doesn't mean I don't find it special that it meant so much to *you* in particular."

Sherry brushed his soft beard. Behind his crooked glasses, he squinted down at her as if he wanted to kiss her and she very much wanted him to. But as much as she wanted to lose herself in his embrace, she came to the North Pole for the biggest story of her career, and she refused to get sidetracked.

Sherry and Nick jumped apart as a group of elves ran past, carrying a tangled mess of Christmas lights.

"Sorry, Nick!" one called out, waving. "We didn't mean to interrupt!"

They giggled, blowing kisses at Nick and Sherry.

"Santa and Sherry sitting in a tree!" Pip skipped. "K-I-S-S-I-N-G!"

"Hush!" Nick yelled.

The elves scurried along, whistling and laughing.

"I'm uh, sorry about that." Nick stroked his beard. "Um, what was that, anyway? I mean, before the elves interrupted us?"

"I don't know." Sherry faked a laugh to ease the tension. "Just us being wrapped up in the moment's magic, I guess."

"Is that all it is?"

"What else could it be?" Sherry gazed at the reindeer, her heart racing. "It's not like we were gonna kiss or something."

"Would that be so strange?"

"Of course!" She faked another laugh, but the tension remained as thick as the snow. "You and me? You're freaking Santa Claus and I'm just... some reporter." She wiggled her toes in her boots. "It wouldn't make any sense."

"I learned a long time ago that a lot in life makes little sense but doesn't mean

it's not real. You've thrown me for a loop, Miss Rice. The more I try to concentrate on the story and not let you get too close, the harder it becomes."

"I understand, but this is bigger than both of us. For you, it's for the kids and for me, it's my career." She tugged on her coat. "I've put in many sleepless nights and hard work to land such a big story, and I can't get distracted."

He sniffled, turning his head away.

"You're a wonderful man. You know that." She touched his arm. "But we gotta

remember what's important."

"You're right." He cleared his throat, reclaiming his composure. "We have to stay on track. Um, I need to go do some work in my office. Want me to walk you

back?"

She smiled. "Sure."

CHAPTER SIX

Sherry settled into the plaid armchair by the window of her room, the heat from her mug of eggnog radiating through her hands.

Snow fell again, blanketing the North Pole in whiteness as Sherry dialed Nina's number and waited for her friend to answer.

The phone rang twice before Nina's cheerful voice came through. "Hey, girl!"

"*Hey*," Sherry sang.

"So, you haven't forgotten my number, after all?"

"Girl, stop." Sherry folded her legs underneath her. "I've called you like five times, but the service gets spotty when it snows and that seems to be every five minutes. I sent you an email."

"Girl, I haven't checked my email in about two months." Nina laughed. "I don't even remember my password anymore. Enough of all this. You're in the North Pole with Santa Claus! Ah! Tell me *everything*!"

"I can't do it justice. I'll have to take some pics so you can see. Oh, wait, this is my room. Hold on." Sherry stood, switched her phone to the video feature and turned around to show Nina every angle of the room. "What do you think?"

"Oh, it's so cute! You even got a little fireplace. It looks so magical."

"You should see Santa's workshop, the village, the elves. Can't explain it." Sherry jumped back in the chair and took a slurp of the creamy eggnog. "This place is everything I imagined and more. It's like stepping into a Christmas movie. The snow, the lights, the decorations—it's like a dream. And yes, I've met plenty of elves, and they're as you'd picture them—tiny, cheerful, and full of energy."

Nina chuckled. "I'm jealous as heck! So, how's the big man himself? Santa's not

giving you too much trouble, is he?"

"Nick?" Sherry hesitated, tapping the side of her mug. "He's... different from what I expected. At first, he was pretty gruff, wanted nothing to do with me. But the more time I spend with him, the more he opens up. He's kind and funny in his own way. And, Nina... there's something else."

"What?"

"Don't you dare laugh."

"Laugh at what?"

"I'm serious, Nina. If you tease me at all, I'm hanging this phone up and I'll never speak to you again."

"I promise I won't laugh. What is it?"

Sherry took a deep breath, not believing what she was about to say. "I think I'm falling for him."

"Who?"

"Santa! I mean, Nick."

"Get the... out of here. You got the hots for Santa Claus? Ha, ha! Y'all been spiking the eggnog or what?"

"See? I knew you'd laugh!"

"I'm not laughing at you, but at the situation. I mean... Sherry, if I'd called you saying the same thing, wouldn't you find it hilarious?"

She grinned, glancing at the grandfather clock in the corner. "I *guess*. Look, I know it sounds crazy, but there's just something about him I can't shake. He's been through so much, and yet, there's still so much good in him. I didn't expect to

feel this way, but here I am."

"Wow, are you serious right now?"

"Yes."

"So what do you wanna do? Be with him? Is the rumor true about Mrs. Claus running off? You wanna be Santa's *rebound*?"

"My mind says I'm crazy and to concentrate on the story, my heart is begging to get closer to him." Sherry wriggled to get more comfortable. "Nina, girl, guess what? Nick almost kissed me today."

"*What*?" Nina cackled. "Man, forget the story you're writing about Santa's *life*. You need to be writing a book about this *romance*. It's unbelievable! Fascinating, but unbelievable."

"If there's ever been a time I needed your advice, it's now. No jokes, Nina."

"If you're falling for Nick, it's okay, because love doesn't always make sense. What matters is how you *feel*. If Nick makes you happy, if he brings out the best in you, then why not give it a shot? Don't overthink it—just go with what feels right. Besides, you need to get on the relationship train again. It's been a year since you had a man."

"Thanks for reminding me." Sherry huffed, sitting back. "Didn't realize you were keeping a tally. I wanna tell him how I feel but scared to death and I don't wanna look silly. I've loved the idea of this man since I was a little girl. How do you go from that to... lust?"

"Lust, huh?" Nina whistled. "Been dreaming of rubbing against that belly and getting a look at them long johns under that suit?"

"Get your mind outta the gutter."

"Ha, ha, ha! You're the one who said 'lust.'"

"Why is life like this? When I was looking for a man, couldn't find a good one
to save my life. Now there's the best man ever right in front of me, but he could
distract me from what's important. I'm not going back to writing about cats and
what causes toe jam, Nina."

"Ewe. Chill, okay. Breathe and don't get stressed out. Whatever happens, just let the chips fall as they may. You got this, girl. Just trust yourself, and trust what you feel. And hey, if things don't work out, at least you'll have one hell of a Christmas story to tell."

Sherry laughed. "Yeah, I guess I will. I'll keep you posted."

"You better call me!"

Sherry hung up and gazed out at the peaceful landscape.

The North Pole, with all its magic, had brought her something she never expected—a chance at love. And for the first time in a long time, she was ready to embrace it.

****

Christmas Eve arrived with a flurry of activity in the village. Excitement packed the air as elves rushed to make final preparations, packing the last of the toys into Santa's sleigh.

The massive wooden contraption gleamed under the soft glow of the lights, its polished runners ready to glide through the snowy sky.

Sherry stood off to the side, happy, but holding a pang of sadness as well. Nick had been more forthcoming than she ever dreamed, so she had tons of fascinating stuff for her story, but the thought of leaving this magical place, and Nick, was heavier than she expected.

Nick approached her, trampling through the snow in his bright-red Santa Claus suit trimmed with gleaming white fur. He'd polished his black boots so well Sherry could see reflections in them and his famous Santa cap sat on top of his head. And to top it off, the biggest smile he'd had since she'd been there lit up his face.

Sherry grinned, sticking her gloved hands into the warmth of her coat. "Wow, you look happy."

"I am!" Nick leaned back as far as he could go, "Ho! Ho! Ho! Merrrrry Christmas!"

Sherry laughed, loving nothing more than hearing his famous salute. "Ready for the big night? Bet you're nervous."

"Ooh, can you tell?" He dropped his shoulders. "Funny how I've been doing this for hundreds of years, and I still get butterflies."

"That's understandable." Sherry observed the elves checking to ensure the reindeer were secured to the sleigh. "You want everything to go perfectly, so you're under a lot of pressure. But you'll be fine, Nick. You can do this in your sleep."

He yawned. "Speaking of sleep, have gotten none in days. But that's the sacrifice." He smiled. "Now you see it, what we've been building up to all year. What do you think?"

Sherry swallowed with her own butterflies fluttering around in her stomach. "Like everything else here, it's magical. You're going to make a lot of kids thrilled tonight. Like you always did *me*. Nick, before you go, I need to say something. I can't keep it to myself anymore."

He scrutinized her with narrow eyes. "What is it, Sherry?"

"Not going to beat around the bush, so might as well get it out." She struggled

to swallow the rocks of anxiety in the middle of her throat. "Nick, I'm falling in love

with you."

CHAPTER SEVEN

Nick's mouth twisted into a pained expression, his eyes boring into hers, as he said nothing in response to Sherry's declaration.

Uh-oh.

Had she made the dumbest mistake of her life? Heck, this hadn't been easy. Sherry didn't just throw out the word "love" to just anyone. For the last few weeks, she'd struggled with this. She thought of Nina's advice to follow her heart and just let the chips fall but now started to regret it.

"I have feelings for you too, Sherry." His deep voice wrapped around her like a hug. "You've become very special. Not just to me, but to this place. Even the elves have fallen in love with you and they're a tough bunch to win over."

She half-chuckled.

"And what you've said..." He gripped her shoulders. "You don't know how much that means to me. But, I'm still hurting because of Gertrude, and it's not fair to start a relationship with you not being over the situation."

"Oh." Sherry's heart sunk. "Are you saying you're still in love with Gertrude?"

"Goodness, no." He let her go. "No, that woman can go jump in a lake for all I

care. But I have to give my heart time to heal so I can trust someone again. How do I know you wouldn't just run off too?"

"Wow. Come on, *Nick*. That's the most insulting thing you've said since I've been here and trust me, you've insulted me a *lot*." She huffed, turning away from him while crossing her arms. "Saying I'm gonna run off. Is that the woman you think I am? I'd never do anything like that. It's not fair to judge other women because of Gertrude."

"Heck, it's not just because of *Gertrude* I'm thinking that." He straightened his

33

gloves. "You're young, beautiful, and got a good head on your shoulders. You want *me*?"

"Yes," she snapped. "I do."

"Until some young buck your age comes along? I'm so old I took classes with Jesus. How could this work?"

"Age is just a number, Nick."

"Yeah, but it's an important one. Age represents time, Sherry." He looked out into the night sky. "No matter what we say, there are things we'll never be able to relate to each other on."

"So? Even if we were the same age or the same race, we'd still have differences. We're supposed to." She laughed. "Couples aren't supposed to match to the T. And I don't care about all that, Nick." She snuggled up to him. "I just want to see where this goes. Nick, I see you. The real you. Isn't that what you want?"

He sighed, avoiding her gaze.

"I'm being selfish." Sherry turned him loose, dropping her head. "This night is about the children, not me. And you're not ready for this."

"It's okay, sweetie." Nick ran his fingers through her braids. "I appreciate you telling me how you feel. It makes tonight even more special."

"Nick!" Pip jumped up and down. "Everything's ready! The reindeer are harnessed, and the sleigh is packed!"

"Hey." Nick clasped Sherry's hands. "You came here to see the *real* Santa Claus,

right? Means you gotta see me in action, then."

She gasped. "What?"

"I've shown you everything except the biggest event of them all." He pinched her cheek. "Sherry, I'd like you to come with me to deliver presents to the kids—"

"Ahhhhhhh!" Sherry fell in the snow and rolled over a million times, howling and screaming. "Oh, ha, ha, ha!" She rolled over on her stomach, punching snow until it flew in her face. "I'm going with Santa Claus. I'm going with freaking Santa to deliver presents! Yay! I can't believe it!"

Nick guffawed, kneeling beside her. "Something tells me you're happy about the invitation."

"Happy? Owww!" She laid on her back, kicking her legs up. "Wow! I can't believe this! This is the dream of every kid in the *world*." She sat up, snow falling from her head. "This is the best Christmas gift ever! I don't know what to say."

"Trust me, you've said quite a lot already." Nick stood and pulled her up. "Are you ready for this? The Christmas Eve of your life?"

"Heck, yes!" She threw her arms around him. "Oh, thank you, Nick. Thank

you so much!"

Nick helped her into the sleigh and climbed in beside her, taking the reins. "Hold on tight," he said with a grin. "This is where the *real* fun begins."

He bellowed his command, and the reindeer leaped forward, the sleigh jolting into motion.

The ground beneath fell away as they soared into the sky, the village shrinking

below until it was just a cluster of twinkling lights.

"Whoa!" Sherry grabbed onto her cap as wind whipped her face. "We're flying, Nick! We're flying!"

"Ho! Ho! Ho! Yes we are!"

Snow-covered forests stretched out below them, glittering like a diamond under the angelic moonlight.

Majestic mountains rose towards the sky, their peaks hidden by a blanket of

stars.

Sherry had never felt so alive and so free. "This is incredible! Woo, hoo!"

Nick's laughter split the sky. "It's different up here, isn't it? Don't you feel free?"

"Yes!"

They soared above the busy cities and quiet towns as Nick steered the sleigh, swooping in low over rooftops to deliver gifts with a flick of his wrist.

Sherry couldn't believe it. She'd seen the magic of Christmas firsthand, and it was more beautiful than she could have ever imagined.

****

Hours later, they returned to the village.

The reindeer, their task complete, shook their heads, spraying snow into the air.

Nick helped Sherry out of the sleigh, both of them quiet, the weight of the night settling in.

The village had fallen into silence as the exhausted elves sought refuge in their

cozy homes.

Sherry grabbed Nick's arms as he held her waist. "Well, that was the best time of my life."

"For me too."

"Oh come on." She scoffed. "You've done this a million times."

"But not with *you*." He squeezed her, making her feel safer than she ever had. "Thank you for coming with me. Seeing you up there was the best Christmas gift I could ask for."

She tingled. "Why?"

"Because the way your face lit up... it was the most beautiful thing I've ever

seen."

"You're Santa, right?"

"Uh..." Nick grinned, switching his eyes left and right. "Either I am or I've been an imposter for millions of years."

Sherry straightened her back. "Well, your job is to give people their Christmas gifts, and you haven't given me *mine*."

He gaped, fidgeting. "Oh, uh... well, I'll be darned." He did a belly-laugh. "No problem. Before you leave, I'll—"

"I want a kiss."

Nick's jaw dropped as the lights on the Christmas trees bathed him and Sherry in sparkles.

A grin crept across his face, revealing those famous dimples that made him even more handsome to her.

The pressure of his hands on her waist felt like a promise, a vow to protect her from any harm.

"Merry Christmas, Sherry." He leaned in close, his bushy beard tickling Sherry's

lips as he pressed them to hers.

Sherry wanted to snatch out her phone and take a picture, knowing no one would ever believe this because even she didn't. She was actually standing here, kissing Santa Claus in the North Pole!

His sweet scent of peppermint forced a tingle throughout her body that filled her with excitement and joy.

CHAPTER EIGHT

The next morning, Sherry woke up feeling both elated and uncertain, the events of the night before replaying in her mind like a dream she wasn't ready to let go of.

She wrapped herself in a thick robe and looked out the window. Everything seemed so calm, so perfect, that she couldn't believe she'd be leaving soon.

She wondered what Nick was doing, the kiss still heavy on her mind as if it had just happened.

The thought of leaving this place, of leaving Nick, crushed her. Besides the story, Sherry hadn't thought coming to the North Pole would change her life in such a profound way, and she couldn't imagine going back to her old life without Nick.

Just as she got downstairs, Nick came in from outside, wiping the bottom of his snowy boots on the rug. "Morning. Or should I say, 'Ho! Ho! Ho! Merrrrryyyy Christmas!"

Sherry hugged him. "Merry Christmas, Nick. Where've you been?"

"Just out checking on the reindeer." Nick shrugged off his coat and hung it by the door. "They needed a little extra care after last night. You okay? Did you sleep well?"

"I'm... I'm fine." She scratched between her braids. "You got a second? I'd like to talk to you."

"Of course."

They took a seat at his card table in the living room.

Nick sat back, looking at her like a parent does when they're about to scold

their kid. "What's on your mind?"

"I was just thinking about..." Sherry ran her hands along the smooth wood.

"What happens next?"

"*Yeah.*" Nick scratched through his beard. "I've been thinking about that, too."

"I don't want to leave." She searched his face for a hint of what he might've been feeling. "But I have a life in Dallas, and I need to see where your story takes me."

He nodded, wiggling his lips.

"But I don't wanna lose what this is and what it *could* be."

The giant Christmas tree by the window sparkled despite its lights not being turned on.

"How can we make this work, Nick?"

"After last night, I don't see how I can go on without you, Sherry, but I'm scared to be hurt again."

"I know how hard it is to trust again."

He reached across the table, taking her hand. "But I wanna try, Sherry. I want to figure this out with *you.*"

"What are you suggesting?"

"We take it one step at a time. There's no rush, no pressure. We figure out what works for us, whether that means visiting each other, or you coming back here... or maybe making a life together."

She squeezed his hand. "How are we going to do this? I live in Dallas and you live here and neither of us can leave our homes."

"If it's important enough, we gotta make it work." He beamed with his cheeks as red as traffic lights. "And you keep acting like the North Pole and Dallas are two separate planets. I can visit you and you can visit me, and perhaps we come up with a more permanent solution down the line."

Sherry groaned, sitting back. "A long distance relationship? Those never work."

"If we work at it, it will. And don't you think what we're feeling is important enough to *try*? Speaking of which..." Nick stood up and pulled her to her feet. "Come on. There's something I want to show you."

She followed him outside and he pulled her past the workshop and the stables until they reached the snowy forest away from the community.

"What is this?"

"Come on."

Their boots crunched through the fallen snow as they made their way along the narrow trail, surrounded by a thicket of bare trees. The air, crisp and biting, coated their lungs with each inhale.

They pushed forward, snapping twigs and branches underfoot until the snowy woods stretched out before them, sparkling in the sunlight like diamonds.

Nick stopped and pointed to a small cottage nestled among the trees, its chimney puffing out a steady stream of smoke.

"That's your place."

"*My* place?"

"For when you visit and so uh..." He pulled her into his arms, smirking. "We can have some alone time without the elves all in our business. I built it a long time ago."

"You mean the *elves* built it a long time ago?"

He huffed. "Same thing."

She laughed.

"No one stays here except for the occasional elf sometimes when his wife kicks

him out after an argument. Other than that, it's just here wasting away."

"So, uh, you're trying to put me up in this cottage, Nick? Like I'm your mistress

or something?"

"Uh, no." He let her go, straightening his posture. "No. Never. I never would do

that—"

"I'm just kidding." She grabbed his shirt. "I love it and this is very sweet."

"Well..." He wiggled his eyebrows. "It's for me too. So we can do what we need to do."

Sherry spit out a laugh. "And what is it we *need* to do, Nick?"

"You know what I mean."

"All right now." She pinched his cheek. "Watch yourself, Santa."

"I might be Santa, but I'm still a man." He wiggled his eyebrows as he clasped her hand in his thick glove.

Sherry trembled like she was back in high school getting ready to do the naughty for the first-first time. This was what she wanted more than anything, but as much as she craved this moment, she couldn't ignore the complications that came

with giving into it.

She'd be leaving soon, and the thought of saying goodbye to Nick was

unbearable. Even to where she didn't even care about the story anymore.

She just wanted to be happy with him.

Nick kissed her forehead. "Come on. Let's go look at the cabin more closely."

Squeezing his hand, Sherry couldn't help but grin as she followed Nick into the cabin.

CHAPTER NINE

Two days later, Sherry stood in Nick's living room, watching as snowflakes drifted past the window. She had a few hours until her flight, so needed to get out of the North Pole in at least the next thirty minutes, but didn't know how she'd walk out that door and leave everything behind.

Nick had been distant since they made love at the cottage and she knew it was because he didn't want to face her leaving. So, he'd retreated to being "professional", hiding his feelings behind that safety net.

The stairs creaked and groaned as Nick came downstairs, his expression surprisingly blank.

He wasn't wearing his glasses and wore a casual outfit with his suspenders, the red suit tucked away until the magic of next Christmas.

"I always wondered..." Sherry turned away from the window. "How do you feel after Christmas is gone?"

He shrugged, popping his suspenders. "No time to 'feel' anything. We spend the entire year getting ready for Christmas, so that's the only thing we focus on, anyway."

"You ever get tired of it? And want a break?"

"Everyone needs a break now and then, but those kids..." He pointed to the window. "Those kids need their toys on Christmas Day, so it's never too early to be prepared."

"You know what I think?" Sherry sauntered past the coffee table. "You hide behind all of this. It's one thing to be dedicated, but you don't need to focus on Christmas every single minute."

"What am I without Christmas, Sherry?" He grimaced. "It's the reason I exist."

"No, you exist to be happy and have a life too, Nick. You can't keep hiding
    behind your workshop and your toys—"

"Let me get Barnaby." He rushed to the front door, passing her suitcases. "You need to get to the airport before you miss your flight—"

"Forget Barnaby, Nick, and stop running."

He kept his back to her, holding onto the door. "*What*?"

"You've been pouting since we left the cottage. Talk to me, Nick."

He slammed the door, shaking the pictures on the walls. "What do you want me to say, huh? That I don't want you to go? Fine, I don't want you to go, Sherry. I want you to stay here with me forever, but so what?" His bald head gleamed in the sunlight streaming through the window. "What's the point of airing this out if it'll get us nowhere? You know what?" He trudged from the door. "Forget the long distance thing. Like you said, it won't work."

Sherry exhaled. "Nick—"

"No, Sherry, no. We've both been dreaming." He stomped past her, walking in circles. "We... we had a wonderful time together, and yes, I am in love with you, too."

Sherry held in tears as she turned to face him.

"But, I can't do this, Sherry. I can't be with you just sometimes and sitting around pining about you when you're not here." He leaned toward the window, pressing his hands on the glass, sniffing. "I want all of you or nothing at all. I can't go through you coming and leaving me once, twice, or three times every year. I can't."

"Okay. Then I'll stay. I'll stay here at the North Pole with you."

"No!" He marched from the window and grabbed her. "No, you won't. I won't

let you give up your life and career for me."

"Nick." She sobbed. "You *are* my life now."

"No, no, no!" He waved left and right. "You forgot about the story? My story

could be your big break and you've worked so hard for it, Sherry." He clasped her face. "I wouldn't forgive myself if I took that away from you."

"But you're not!" She grabbed his suspenders. "I know what I'm saying and the other stuff's not important anymore. Don't you see, Nick? For years, all I worried about was 'making it big as a reporter' but that's because I had nothing else in my life. Nina told me all the time how I'd regret looking back on life and not being in love, but I was afraid of getting hurt and I didn't even wanna try. But, Nick... you mean more to me than any story. I'd be the happiest woman in the world just being here in the North Pole with you."

His face twisted as a tear fell.

"This is what I want, Nick. You're *what* I want." She pulled him into a tender kiss that shook everything around them. "We could have a magical life together. I... I can help with the toys, keep the home fires burning while you work, just... every day would be like a dream. What do you say, Nick?" She shook him. "What do you *say*?"

"I..." He let her go. "I say 'no', Sherry. You're a young, beautiful woman with your whole life ahead of you. I'm not letting you throw that away to sit around here. Besides, you'd be bored here in a week."

"I've been here for weeks and haven't gotten bored. I love it here, Nick."

"That's 'cause you don't live here. But if you had to deal with this every day...

no. It's mundane here, Sherry. We do the same thing over and over. It's exciting to

you now, but once you got used to it, you might end up resenting it."

"No way." She shook her head. "I could never resent this place."

"What about your parents? Nina? You're just gonna leave them?"

"Like you always say, this is the North Pole, Nick, not Mars. They can visit me and I can visit them. Why are you making excuses?"

"Your flight." He tapped his watch. "Your plane leaves soon and you're gonna be on it."

"No, I won't."

"Yes, you will." He marched to the front door and grabbed her suitcases. "Come on, Sherry. Time to go."

She barged up to him in her knitted pom pom beanie hat that matched her gloves. "I'm not leaving until you look me in the eye and tell me you really want me to leave."

He took a deep breath before meeting her eyes. "Please, Sherry. I... I want you to go. Live your life and forget me." His voice cracked. "At least until next Christmas."

"Liar!" She hit him in the stomach. "I thought Santa wasn't supposed to lie! I thought you're supposed to make everyone's dreams come true but you're taking mine! I love you, Nick. Don't do this. Don't tear us apart like this, please."

He turned his head away. "Have a safe trip, Sherry. I'll walk you to the sleigh—"

"Don't bother." She snatched her suitcases from him. "I know the way."

Sherry stormed past Nick and charged through the deep snow without

looking back.

CHAPTER TEN

Back in Dallas, Sherry and Nina paced in front of Ms. Ray's office as she read Sherry's Santa story. Sherry peeked through the glass to see Ms. Ray focused as ever, flipping through the type-written document as she scanned every word. Ms. Ray was old-school, so she liked to read the big stories as hard copies. She claimed she got more involved with the story that way.

Whatever the case, Sherry just hoped she'd hurry the heck up.

"Man." Sherry leaned against the glass. "I haven't been this nervous since my last pregnancy test. What's taking her so long?"

"Her being slow is a good thing." Nina sucked on a cream swirl lollipop. "Means something in its interesting her or she wouldn't have gone past the first page. You're going to be fine. That story was a killer. I read it and I know a good story. Just wish you'd have taken my advice."

"I would never put in there that Nick and I had sex."

"Why not, *girl*?" Nina cackled. "Heck, if you wanna fly to the top, saying you got it on with Santa would've done the trick."

"Nick isn't some prop for me to use. I care about him." Sherry glanced at the tile floor. "I miss him. Can't stop thinking about him. You said if I let the chips fall, everything would work out. It didn't."

"Just because you're not together now doesn't mean you won't be." Nina slurped on the candy. "Cheer up. You've been moping since you got back. Where's that pretty smile—"

"Rice," Ms. Ray bellowed. "Get in here! Now!"

Sherry exhaled. "Goodness."

Nina hugged her. "You got this, girl. If you believe it, it'll happen."

Unconvinced, Sherry nodded, then entered Ms. Rice's office and sat down.

Ms. Rice sat across from her desk, peering at Sherry through her thick reading glasses and all Sherry could do was prepare herself for the firestorm Ms. Ray was about to unleash because somehow, somewhere, Sherry had botched this whole thing.

"All these years, you wanted the 'big story.'" Ms. Ray snatched off her glasses. "The one that would make you a star."

Sherry squirmed.

"You always felt like this place was too big for you. Like I was wasting your talent."

"I'm very grateful for the chance you gave me, Ms. Ray. Never said I wasn't."

"You know how you show me appreciation, Sherry?" Ms. Ray leaned forward, clasping her hands. "You show me by taking an opportunity I give you and turning it into gold."

"You don't have to say anymore." Sherry relaxed her shoulders. "You didn't like the story, but I worked hard on it and it's full of passion. I didn't dictate things like I usually do. I let Nick just talk about things, teach me, and show me his world and I wrote about things from his eyes. Isn't that why you gave me this assignment? Isn't this why Nick did it? So people could see the real him? Huh?" She stood, sniffling. "But like everything else, I screw this up, too. Just fire me, Ms. Ray. I don't have what it takes to make it in this business if I could mess this up—"

"Sherry, shut up."

Sherry stopped. "Yes, ma'am."

"Before you go degrading yourself and your talents, can I talk?" Ms. Ray reclined in her chair. "Sherry, I wanted gold. I wanted you to prove you had the chops

and you did that girl! Ha, ha! You did it!"

"Uh, what?"

"This was amazing." Ms. Ray grabbed the document. "It's better than I thought it could ever be. Sherry, this story... this story, it's gonna catapult you to heights you can't even imagine. Every major outlet is going to want a piece of you after this."

Sherry gasped, covering her mouth.

"Sherry, I'm talking New York, California, hell CBS, ABC, NBC, they're all gonna want you."

"Oh, my God!" Sherry grabbed the arms of her chair. "Oh, my loving God. Are you for real?"

"TV appearances, book deals—you name it. And wait until it goes crazy on TikTok. It's a piece everyone can love from the young to the old. Men and women, any nationality and race. I've never read a story that so many people could relate to."

"Well, that's because he's Santa Claus!" Sherry laughed. "Not me."

"But it's your words that brought this to life. Sherry, you've given people something no one ever has... Santa Claus in his purest, most vulnerable, most exposed form. I tell you." Ms. Ray shook her head, chuckling. "You're going to be the next Barbara Walters with *this*. The Barbara Walters of the new generation."

"Barbara Walters? I... I don't know what to say! I..." Overwhelmed by emotion, Sherry burst into tears, caught off guard by her own reaction.

"What in the *world?* Sherry, what's gotten into you?"

"I'm happy, don't get me wrong, but what's the point of all this if I'm going to be alone? If I have to give up on love?"

"Ah, that." Ms. Ray set the document down. "Every career-driven woman goes

through this at some point. You're at a crossroads where you feel you've sacrificed

your romantic life for your career."

"Haven't I? Look at you. You started the *Dallas Daily* when you were only

twenty-two and had no help from anyone. Went through sexism and all the other crap. You even said people didn't wanna write for your paper when you first started because you're a woman."

"That's right."

"I admire you so much, but then I look at the rest of your life. Ugh."

Ms. Ray scowled. "Excuse me?"

"You never got married. Never had kids. Been single for about thirty years. No offense, but I don't wanna end up like that."

"I beg your pardon!" Ms. Ray sat up. "Oh, so you see me as some old spinster who chose her career over her life? Let me tell you something, Miss Thinks-She-Knows-Everything-About-My-Life. I never got married because I didn't *want* to get married!" She wiggled her neck. "I had proposals coming from men left and right who would've moved heaven and earth for me, but I didn't wanna be second fiddle to no man and give up the stuff I worked hard for. And why the hell I wanna be married to have some man try to tell me what I can and can't do? No! Honey, I can get up and go anywhere I want, not having to worry about nobody else. If I wanna take a vacation to Tahiti for two months, I can get up and go. Marriage? Girl, please."

"Damn it, I'm an idiot. I didn't mean it like that—"

"And as for kids? Sherry, I can't believe this backwards thinking is coming from you. I didn't have kids because I didn't want the little brats. Now what? You're talking like these men who wanna take us back to the fifties. Like I gave up so much because I dared to choose a life that revolves around *myself* and not everyone else in the world."

"Yes, you're right, I—".

"I didn't *give* up anything. I chose a career on its own, and I like my life very much. I also get my share of men, thank you very much, missy."

"Forgive me. I'm so sorry, Ms. Ray. I didn't mean to offend you. I'm ashamed of what I just said."

"Don't pity me because I don't need it. You might see some lonely old woman

with no life outside of this place, but it's not true. And even if it was, it would be my decision. Plenty of women have a career and are married and have kids. Women can do both and we can also choose not to. For goodness sakes, Sherry."

"Please, please. Forget what I said." Sherry waved her hands from side to side. "You know I didn't mean it that way. I'm all for the independent woman. No, a woman doesn't need kids or a husband to be happy, but I thought I was like that, but now I'm not. I want the husband, kids, and the career too."

"Well, go get it then! You know what your problem is? You work hard, but you expect just because you work hard you'll get things easier. Hate to say it, Sherry, but the world is not fair. Many people work their butts off and get nowhere. The world doesn't owe you a darn thing."

"You're right. But I pushed people away, convinced myself that success was the only thing that mattered. Now I know better. For *me*, I mean. It's hard, you know?" Sherry took out a napkin and dabbed her damp eyes. "My fear is I'll achieve everything I set out to do, but won't have no one to share it with. It's an empty feeling."

"We all gotta live our own paths, and you need to do what makes *you* happy. Think about what matters to *you*, Sherry. And whatever you decide, know that you've earned every bit of success coming your way. But don't be afraid to follow your heart,

too."

CHAPTER ELEVEN

Nick stood in the middle of his workshop, overseeing the busy elves assembling toys for the next Christmas. The elves scurried back and forth, some tinkering with dollhouses, others putting the final touches on shiny new bicycles. The usual buzz took Nick's mind off of whatever was bothering him, but he just couldn't get Sherry out of his mind.

Everywhere he looked, he thought of the kiss, the passion they shared at the cottage, and how she embodied the genuine spirit of everything important to him.

He cracked his knuckles, the weight of his regret settling on his shoulders. He should have let her stay, married her and made her a part of his life forever. But he'd let fear and doubt guide his actions, pushing her away when all he wanted was to pull her closer.

"Nick?" Barnaby stood beside him, his eyes lit up with concern for his boss. "You've been standing in the same spot for an hour. Haven't so much as even grunted let alone talk."

Nick coughed out a chuckle. "And you've been watching me long enough to notice, huh? Sorry, Barnaby. Just got a lot on my mind."

"This wouldn't have anything to do with a certain reporter, would it?"

Nick straightened his shoulders. "I don't know what you're talking about."

"You're a terrible liar, Nick. That's because you never do it." Barnaby smiled. "I'm talking about that young, beautiful reporter who turned your world upside down. That one."

"I messed up, didn't I? I thought letting her go was the right thing, but I've never felt this empty. Not even when Gertrude ran off. I don't know what to do."

"Well, you're not the first to let fear impede something good. But that doesn't mean you can't make it right."

"And how do I do that?"

"The only way *you* can." Barnaby put his hand on Nick's shoulder. "You're Santa, remember? You're the guy who brings joy to the world. If anyone knows how to make things right, it's you. But you have to make a move before it's too late."

"How do I know it's not already?"

"Because she still loves you *now*." Barnaby crossed his arms, shrugging. "But if you wait too long, she might not anymore. You've got a sleigh and reindeer that can fly faster than the speed of light. There's nothing stopping you from going after her, Nick. But you have to take that risk."

The thought of seeing Sherry again, of holding her in his arms and telling her how he felt, filled Nick with a sense of urgency he hadn't felt in years.

"It's a new year, Nick." Barnaby waved his arm around. "Do you wanna spend it lonely or in love?"

"You're right. I've spent centuries making dreams come true for others—maybe it's time I fought for my own. Tell the elves to get the reindeer and sleigh ready. I'm going to Texas!"

****

"Girl, you can't be serious." Nina breathed through the phone that night, muffling Sherry's ear. "Sherry, you're nuts."

"Maybe." Sherry lay on her bed, gorging on spicy tortilla chips with her Bluetooth earbud on. "But I miss him, and I'll only truly be happy with *him*."

"But *moving* to the North Pole? Wow. Uh... just wow. Your career is about to go through the roof! You wanna uproot now?"

"I can have my career in the North Pole, and maybe I'll even start my paper

there. I just know life without Nick by my side isn't worth it."

Nina let out a deep sigh. "I'd hate it if you left, but I get it. After all, I'm the one who's been pushing you to get a man. I'm happy for you and got your back always."

"Thanks, Nina. I just have to do what's in my heart, you know? But I got a lot to do first. Gotta talk to Mom and Dad too. Not looking forward to *that*."

"Yeah, your momma's gonna flip."

"Well, she'll have to accept it." Sherry bit a chip. "It's my life, and I have to live it how I see fit."

"Wow, just. Woo. This is a big step, but I'll be here to help you with anything you need—"

"What's that?" Sherry threw down her chips and scampered to the window at the sudden commotion outside.

Her neighbors ran through the streets, yelling and pointing at the night sky.

Sherry leaned out her window, spotting a magical sight - Nick, with his unruly beard, yelling commands as his reindeer soared through the darkness surrounded by a beam of light, the bells around the reindeer' necks getting louder as they approached.

Sherry jumped up and down on the carpet. "Oh my God!"

"What?" Nina shouted into Sherry's ear. "What's going on?"

"Girl, you won't believe this!" Sherry sweated under her headscarf. "Nick is here! He's here, look!" She got her phone and videoed the spectacle for Nina to see.

"Oh, wow!" Nina laughed. "That's incredible!"

"Ho! Ho! Ho!" Nick halted the reindeer right onto Sherry's front lawn.

The people snapped pictures while howling and jumping.

"Hey, it's Santa!" Sherry's neighbor's little ten-year-old daughter pointed at the boisterous Nick. "Santa!"

Nick roared with laughter, waving at the stunned public. "Sherry!" He stomped toward the house. "Sherry, wake up! It's Nick!"

"Nina, I have to go!" Sherry snatched the earpiece out of her ear and ran to the front door, flinging it open just as Nick got to her walkway.

He towered over everyone like a 100-year-old oak tree, his shoulders squared with confidence, and his smile radiating in her porch light.

"Nick!" She locked her arms around his portly middle. "Oh, I can't believe you're here! I missed you so much."

He squeezed her into a hug. "I'm so sorry for pushing you away and for not fighting for us. But I love you, Sherry. I love you more than I've ever loved anything in my life."

Sherry sniffled, her body quaking with emotion and adrenaline. "I love you too, Nick. I shouldn't have ever left so it was my fault too!"

"Sh." He laid his gloved fingertip on her lips. "Ditch the blame game. We both made mistakes, but what's important is that I'm here for you now, Sherry!" He picked her up and twirled her around, cheers and applause growing louder as more people joined the crowd. "I love you, Sherry, and I want everyone to know it!" He put her down, huffing and puffing. "Before you left, you said you wanted to live in the North Pole with me. Does that offer still stand?"

"Oh, you bet your big jolly butt it does!" She grabbed him into a sloppy kiss and the crowd howled. "I wanna be with you now more than before."

"That makes me the happiest man in the world, but the only way I'll accept

that is if we make it official."

Sherry gaped. "What do you—"

Nick dropped down on one knee in the grass, his hand shaking as he took her

trembling fingers in his.

The crowd went quiet as they watched Nick and Sherry with wide eyes and opened mouths.

"Oh my God." Sherry struggled to catch her breath, her legs shaking as if they were about to fall off.

"I don't have a ring yet, but I can't wait, Sherry." Nick squeezed her hand as he looked up into her eyes. "Sherry...uh, what's your middle name?"

She muttered, "Phyllis."

He grimaced. "*Phyllis?*"

"I'm named after my great aunt. Shut up!"

Snickering, Nick continued, "Sherry Phyllis Rice, will you marry me and make me happier than no man's ever been while allowing me to spend the rest of my life making *you* happy too?"

"Heck yes!" She dropped to her knees and hugged him. "I'll marry you, Nick! Oh, I'm so happy!"

The audience cheered and clapped, dancing along to the lively tune of the reindeer bells.

"Well!" Sherry twirled, dancing to the jingling. "Can't nobody say you don't

know how to bring a party!"

"Yeah, don't let the old age fool ya." Nick swayed, then did a booty-bump with Sherry. "I know how to party! Especially when someone's spiked the eggnog."

They laughed.

"And I got great news." Sherry grabbed him. "Ms. Ray loved your story, and she

thinks it'll make me famous!"

"That's wonderful, honey." Nick twirled Sherry around. "I knew you'd do great."

"But it's because of you, Nick." She threw herself up against his soft warmness. "You made my dreams come true. In more ways than you know."

Nick looked toward the block party that had broken out. "Why don't you say we leave them to celebrate and you show me around your place?"

"You got it." Sherry smirked, taking his hand. "What room would you like to see first?"

Nick dipped his head, looking at her over his glasses. "You know the one."

"The bedroom it is!"

Sherry pulled him inside and shut the door.

THE END

Thanks so much for choosing my book! I would be very appreciative if you would leave a rating or a review. Much love!

To receive book announcements subscribe to Stacy's mailing list:

Mailing List[1]

---

1.   https://stacybooks.eo.page/cjjy6

MORE CHRISTMAS ROMANCES:

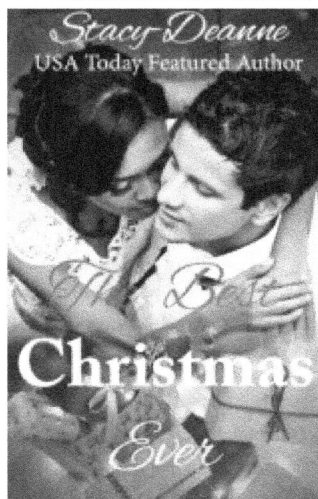

AVAILABLE HERE: http://amzn.to/2BSu1tf

Don't miss out!

Visit the website below and you can sign up to receive emails whenever Stacy-Deanne publishes a new book. There's no charge and no obligation.

https://books2read.com/r/B-A-RTFC-HZLWE

BOOKS 2 READ

Connecting independent readers to independent writers.

Also by Stacy-Deanne

The Weekend
The Gramophone
Sunday Meal
Sex in the Wild West 10-Book Bundle
The Barracuda
The Man in the Painting
Hannah's Gift
Lost Souls
Shared At His Command
Taken

Sinful Secrets
Dead Weight
Oleander
Paradise
Fatal Deception

Stripped Romantic Suspense Series
Stripped
Captured
Damaged
Haunted
Possessed
Destined
Stripped Series Books 1-3
Stripped Series (Books 4-6)

Tate Valley Romantic Suspense Series

Now or Never
Chasing Forever
Sinner's Paradise
Last Dance
Tate Valley The Complete Series

The Bruised Series
Bruised
Captivated
Disturbed
Entangled
Twisted

The Good Girls and Bad Boys Series
Who's That Girl?
You Know My Name
Hate the Game

The Mistresses of Rose Lake
The Mistress of Deveraux
The Mistress of Bannister

The Studs of Clear Creek County
The White Knight Cowboy
The Forlorn Cowboy
The Lavish Cowboy

The Lovelorn Cowboy
The Reluctant Suitor

Standalone
Gonna Make You Mine
Empty
Gonna Make You Mine
A Matter of Time
Harm a Fly
Harm a Fly
You're the One
Worth the Risk
Seven's Deadly Sins
Hawaii Christmas Baby
Sometimes Money Ain't Enough
The Best Christmas Ever
Prey
The Good Girls and Bad Boys Series
Bruised Complete Series
Tate Valley Complete Series
The Princess and the Thief
The Little Girl
The Stranger
Seducing Her Father's Enemy
Stalked by the Quarterback
Secrets of the Heart
Five Days
Off the Grid
Sex in Kenya
A Cowboy's Debt
Billionaires for Black Girls Set (1-4)

A Savior for Christmas
The Samsville Setup
Trick The Treat
The Cowboy She Left in Wyoming
Theodore's Ring
Wrangle Me, Cowboy
The Billionaire's Slave
The Cowboy's Twin
Everwood County Plantation
Billionaires for Black Girls Set 5-7
The Lonely Hearts of San Sity
Stranded with Billionaire Grumpy Pants
An Alpha For Christmas
Stalked by the Devil
Her North Pole Affair

Milton Keynes UK
Ingram Content Group UK Ltd.
UKHW031122081124
450926UK00001B/50